NICK JR

The BACKYARDIGANS™

Trouble on the Train

by Catherine Lukas
illustrated by The Artifact Group

Ready-to-Read

SIMON SPOTLIGHT/NICK JR.
New York   London   Toronto   Sydney

Based on the TV series *Nick Jr. The Backyardigans*™ as seen on Nick Jr.®

SIMON SPOTLIGHT
An imprint of Simon & Schuster Children's Publishing Division
1230 Avenue of the Americas, New York, New York 10020
Manufactured in the United States of America
First Edition
2 4 6 8 10 9 7 5 3 1
Cataloging-in-Publication Data for this book is available from the Library of Congress.
ISBN-13: 978-1-4169-2818-8
ISBN-10: 1-4169-2818-9

Cowboy and Cowgirl
AUSTIN UNIQUA

take a break from herding cows.

"Here comes a ,"
TRAIN

says Cowgirl .
UNIQUA

"That  is carrying
TRAIN

a BOTTLE of barbecue sauce,"

says Cowgirl UNIQUA .

"The sauce is on its way to

Cooking Cowboy .

TYRONE

He makes the best

 in the West!"

BURGERS

Someone else

is watching the too.
TRAIN

"Ready to rob that ,
TRAIN

Bandit  ?"
PABLO

asks Bandit .
TASHA

"Yes I am, Bandit ,"
TASHA

says Bandit .
PABLO

"I hear there is a
BOTTLE

of special sauce on that !"
TRAIN

says Bandit .
PABLO

"I will use this  ROPE

to try to grab the BOTTLE !"

says Bandit TASHA.

"If we get that 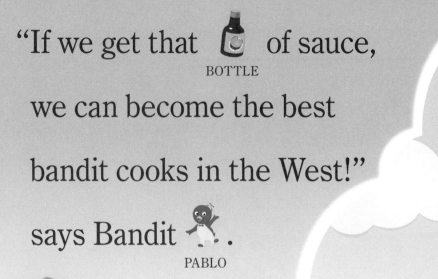 of sauce,
BOTTLE

we can become the best

bandit cooks in the West!"

says Bandit .
PABLO

Bandit  twirls her .
TASHA   ROPE

She throws it through the .
                                WINDOW

She lassoes the  !

BOTTLE

"Look! Bandits!"
says Cowboy .
AUSTIN
"They just stole the  !"
BOTTLE

"After them!"

says Cowgirl .

UNIQUA

Cowboy  and Cowgirl

AUSTIN   UNIQUA

hop onto their  .

HORSES

They chase the bandits.

"Watch out!"

yells Bandit .
TASHA

"  in the road!"
PICKLES

It is too late.

Bandit  and his PABLO HORSE

skid and slide on the PICKLES.

Bandit drops the 🍼 .
PABLO   BOTTLE

Cowgirl 🦎 catches it.
         UNIQUA

"Good work!"

says a voice.

It is Cooking Cowboy  !

TYRONE

"We just wanted to be

the best bandit cooks

in the West,"

says Bandit  sadly.
TASHA

"You do not need to be bandits!"

says Cooking Cowboy 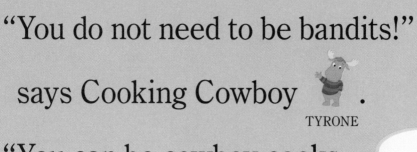.

TYRONE

"You can be cowboy cooks

with me instead!"

"Yes, sir," says Cowgirl . "These surely are the best  BURGERS in the West!"